laundry

DAZE

A NOVELLA

TANZANIA GLOVER

without the prior written permission of the publisher, except in the case of brief quotations embodied in critical reviews and certain other noncommercial uses permitted by copyright law. This book or any portion thereof may not be reproduced or used in any manner without the express written permission of the writer or publisher. The use of brief quotations is allowed in book reviews.

Cover Art by New Levels Graphics

www.tanzaniaglover.com

Booking With Love
332 S Michigan Ave

TANZANIA GLOVER

Suite #121- 2217
Chicago, IL 60604
www.bookingwithlove.com

I dedicate this to Blaze Hawkins because she's the one who wouldn't take her foot off of my neck for delaying the last book in The Soundtrack Series and the end result is the following novella.

Thank you Chef B!

Enjoy and don't forget to check out the playlist that complements this story!

Sidney

Daren Harris had only been my neighbor for about a year and a half, but in that short amount of time I had gotten to know her better than most. I knew what her favorite foods were because she always had the hallways in our building smelling like a barbecue joint. I knew what music she listened to when she cleaned up because it came blasting through the walls every Sunday morning like clockwork.

But the one thing that I knew better than anybody was how particular she was about her laundry.

She was the only person I knew who actually followed the instructions from the tags on clothes and she even had a little mesh bag for her delicates so I never really got to see the pretty panties and bras that I knew she wore. And if by chance she ran out of her bougie ass detergent and fabric softener she wouldn't do laundry at all until she got more delivered from online. That's why I eventually started using the same brand as her so she would never have any reason to cancel laundry day with me.

After a while I had to admit that it was worth the price because my clothes always looked new and the scent it left on me was subtle but intoxicating. It reminded me of her. And sometimes when I was having a bad day I would pull my collar over to my nose to remind myself that it was only a day or two away before I got to spend a couple uninterrupted hours with her.

And even though I wasn't anywhere close to being her man, it didn't matter because on Wednesday nights it felt like she was mine. But it was too bad that as soon as we were done folding sheets and matching socks reality kicked back in.

And it didn't matter how deep the conversation had gotten or how much I'd made her laugh. I was always reminded that I was just her friend. Hell lower than a friend. I was just her neighbor who, almost two years ago now, was naïve enough to think that I could be around her on a consistent basis and not eventually fall for everything that was great about her, which was everything about her.

Doing laundry together might not have been a big deal to most people, but it had always been more than just another chore to me. Back in the day when it was just me and my mama we would go to the laundromat in our neighborhood together and it was always an adventure. We would listen to dusties, dance, and she would chase me all throughout the place and let me ride in the carts. Looking back through grown man eyes, I was sure that it was just something else she had to do on her own since my pops had left, but I liked how it didn't seem like a burden because we always had each other.

That's why when I decided to move to California a couple years ago I bought her a washer and dryer out of my savings so she wouldn't have to go there without me anymore. And I guess in a weird way I'd created the same thing with Daren only instead of just having fun with my mama while the clothes were in I was unintentionally falling for her.

But I wasn't happy about it and if I could I would have gone back to the beginning and undid everything that had gotten me caught up with her. I was too young to be settling down and I wanted to live like a rock star for at least a few years before having to eventually get my shit together. But I knew that wasn't an option because being in love with a girl like Daren meant having to step up to the plate and be a man.

I still remembered the first time I had gotten roped into the whole laundry thing with her since it wasn't that long after she had moved in. I'd known I had a new neighbor for weeks by then because of the sound of a hammer hitting nails into our shared wall and all the good smelling food lately, but at that point I hadn't actually seen her yet. It wasn't until after work one day when I came across an unfamiliar brown skinned woman struggling to get a big bag of laundry up to the top floor that I knew it had to be her since I knew everybody else in the building.

I was tired from a long day and my own big heavy bag of mail that I'd been lugging around for my eight hour shift at the post office, but I was still about to handle it for her since I never passed up the chance to do a good deed because I was a firm believer in karma. Well that and I was glad to finally see somebody else my age on the floor because she looked like she was about mid-twenties like me.

"Hey let me get that for you." I hadn't even bothered waiting for her to agree and just took it from her then threw it over my shoulder like I was black Santa.

She let out a small *thank you* which caused me to look back at her for a second because the mousy, almost childlike voice didn't exactly match her appearance.

"As much as I would love to pretend like I had it, I really didn't," she added through an exhausted laugh then wiped her damp forehead.

She was exaggerating because it wasn't as heavy as it looked, but she didn't seem like the working out type so obviously I could handle it better than she could.

"Right here is fine," she said when we got to the top floor, but I continued walking it down the hall to sit in front of her door. "Thanks again. I'm Daren by the way." Her extended hand reached out for mine, but it wasn't until I took it that we both really took a good look at each other.

She was shorter than average and wearing a heavy beige sweater that looked like it was swallowing her so I couldn't see much of her pudgy body, but she had a cute round face and a warm, inviting smile.

"I'm Sid and I guess we're neighbors," I told her as I nodded over to my door.

"Oh so you're the guy who keeps playing all of those loud instrumentals on weekends?" she said with playfulness lacing her complaint even though I could see her avoiding making too much eye contact with me.

"Yeah I'm a producer so I have to hear if it really knocks for a minute, but you can always let me know if it's bothering you too much."

"It's no problem. I'm sure you noticed me paying you back with my gospel music on Sunday mornings."

"Yeah I did. I actually figured you were an older church lady type like Ms. Gwen on the other side of me," I told her as I was about to point to the door before realizing that we were still holding onto each other's hands. She quickly let go then nervously laughed as she placed her hand at her side.

"No. Lord knows I'm far from a holy roller. It's just a habit I picked up from my mama and grandma. According to them a house isn't really clean unless Shirley Caesar's hollering in the background, you know?"

"Maybe that explains why my spot looks like it does," I told her as I finally unlocked my door. It was the perfect opportunity to naturally end the conversation and I was actually halfway inside when I suddenly decided to go for karma galore today.

"Daren?" I called out to her right before she was about to close her door too.

"Yeah?" she asked and we shared a smile because instead of stepping back into the hall we had both just poked our heads out.

"I try to do laundry most Wednesdays around seven because nobody's ever really in there then. If you do yours at the same time I could bring your stuff up for you again."

"That's nice of you, but you don't have to do that. Shoot I need to be trying to lift some weights or something to get in better shape," she said before messing around with a loose string on her sweater.

"I don't mind. And you really shouldn't be down in the basement by yourself too much," I warned her because even though we didn't live in the roughest neighborhood in Inglewood, it wasn't the best either. "Shit I don't even like being down there by myself for too long."

"Are you sure?" she asked again like she couldn't believe the offer was sincere, but I assured her it was. "Okay. It's a date then. See you next week."

"Cool. Have a good night." Right when I went to shut the door I heard her call my name.

"Sid?"

"Yeah?"

"I didn't mean it like it would be a *date* date. I was just you know, using the saying *'It's a date'*. But I know it's not a real date or anything like that."

"Nah you're good. I knew what you meant."

"Okay because I'm sort of an overthinker and I would have been replaying that in my head all night like *'Does he think this is a date? Because I don't think this is a date.'* Not that I wouldn't date you. Just that I knew it wouldn't be a date. And not that I think that you would even want to date me, but--" she managed to ramble off before I finally put her out of her misery.

"Daren, calm down. It's just laundry. We're not getting married."

"Right. Okay. Sorry about that," she said with a shy smile before hurrying inside.

That first laundry date we had mostly just talked about where we were from and how we had ended up in California. I was surprised to find out that she was a fresh transplant from Vermont because I didn't even know they had black people up there. And when she learned I was from Chicago she just wanted to know if I had ever seen anybody get shot before because death and deep dish pizza was all she knew about the city. I was actually from the 'burbs though so I didn't have any newsworthy stories to share.

The next Wednesday she'd brought a deck of cards down with her because I told her that I could teach her how to play two-hand Spades. And by the time our clothes were dry I had her coming out of her shell some and slamming the cards down like she had been playing all of her life.

By week three I was comfortable enough to bring her a

couple of my edibles to try to get her to relax because already I could tell that she wasn't just an overthinker. I wasn't a psychologist but anybody with eyes could have diagnosed her with some type of anxiety. They actually got the job done too and she swore she had never slept better that night the next time I saw her.

Before I knew it Wednesdays had gone from hump day to my favorite day of the week because there was always something interesting to talk about with my new favorite neighbor. And after a while I didn't even bother waiting around for Wednesdays anymore. I would just knock on her door to tell her something funny I'd heard before I forgot it. And while an edible a day kept her nerves in check she was still really shy so we would just stand in her doorway for a minute or two each time.

But the first time she invited me in for dinner it was over with. I had already been smelling everything from next door but getting to see and taste her food had me feeling like I was back home. After that I made her drop that shy shit with me because that's when I had decided we were about to be cool *for real* for real. At least once a week I would call her from the grocery store asking her what to buy because as long as she could throw down like that she would always have a friend in me.

It was a cool little situation for a while too and it worked because neither of us had any ulterior motives to being around each other. It was just convenient and fun since we were both new to the state, we didn't really know anybody else like that, and we didn't plan on living there too long because we had the nerve to be out here dream chasing like Meek.

I delivered mail by day and produced as SidTheKid by night

while she did hair at a salon not too far from here. My beats were getting better with time and she had even started picking up a few noteworthy clients since her ultimate goal was to do hair for celebrities.

You couldn't tell by looking at her simple ponytail wearing ass, but she really was good at what she did. And she could even do a little makeup too because I had seen women come by her spot looking rougher than a mug then leave looking like a model. I always wondered why she never did herself up too since she clearly knew how to, but I liked that she wasn't superficial like most LA girls. She was just cute in a laidback kind of way.

After a while everybody in the building assumed we must've had something going on especially Ms. Gwen who would always smile when she saw us together. But I knew that would never happen because I had only been focused on getting my beats into the right hands then. And I'd told myself when I did decide to get a girl she definitely wouldn't be the girl next door type because after living out here for a little while I had gotten used to certain standards that a woman like Daren just didn't live up to.

And I mean it wasn't like I was a pretty boy or something either, but a young nigga was handsome. And besides it was a guarantee that when the real money started coming in from producing I would want an upgrade anyway so I stayed single and just fucked around here and there. No woman would ever be able to say I got dough and changed or left her for a golddigger because I was holding out and saving up to be able to afford the golddiggers. Real talk just like Simba, I couldn't wait to be king either.

But at the drop of a hat I got the wind knocked out of me when

Daren started hanging with the other hairstylists from the salon. They had her going to ratchet clubs and dipping in her savings to buy clothes and shit I knew she couldn't afford by the look of her beat up old phone and hoopty. I wasn't happy with them taking her away from me so much, but it was good to see her lightening up, making friends and not being so damn tense and wound up all the time.

But unfortunately that was just the beginning and the new clothes eventually led to a head to toe makeover that then led to a pep in her step that started attracting attention from niggas that I had seen walk right past her before. And they weren't just doing a double take either. They were doubling back and trying to get her number too. I didn't like that shit. She was supposed to always be my sweet lil shy neighbor Daren not *trying to be cute for these niggas and the 'gram* Daren.

I did find some relief when I realized that even though she looked different on the outside, she was still the same on the inside. She obviously loved all the attention that her new look got her, but every time somebody would step to her she still ended up turning them all down. Well almost all of them.

About six months ago I had knocked on her door to see if she was home. It was a Wednesday like any other, but I was just getting off of work and after weeks of finessing I'd finally gotten a **bad** little thing to agree to come over so I was gonna try to get Daren to hold off on laundry until the following week.

I knocked a couple times then gave up figuring she must have been out, but before I could get too far a tall stocky dude opened up. I double checked the number on the door to make sure I had the right place and of course

I did because she lived in 5C and I was in 5B. Off top I knew he wasn't a relative because I had seen pictures of her brother and her dad and neither was as tall or as dark as this nigga was.

And even though he had locs he couldn't have been a client either because she only did men's hair at the salon. I didn't even know why but realizing that he was most likely there for pleasure and not business instantly made my face frown up and my body tense.

"You need me to sign for something?" he asked after I just stood there for a second looking at him. I was still in my blue uniform so I knew he wasn't necessarily trying to be funny, but I still mean mugged his goofy ass anyway.

"Where's Daren?" I asked without clearing my throat like I needed to because I wanted him to hear that extra grit in my voice.

"Ay D, the mailman's got something for you," he said summoning her over from the bathroom. She was all smiles as she approached *and* not dressed in her usual sweats for laundry night in a little while either.

"No this is Sidney, the neighbor I told you about who--"

"Sid," I corrected her because she knew better than to use my government name in front of a nigga I didn't know.

With her small hand on his back she turned to formally introduce him to me. "Right. My bad *Sid*. This is my uh…my date Zeke."

A'ight so boom. I was far from a rowdy nigga and it hadn't actually been *on sight* with anybody in years, but instantly I wanted to get a hold of homie's locs then stomp him out at the way she had smiled up at him when she said his name. It was the same way that she'd smiled at me the day we met and it wasn't until then that I realized just how much I missed that version of her.

"This is your friend with the beats?" he asked her as he reached out to dap me, but I looked at his hand for a while before returning the gesture. I couldn't explain where all the hostility was coming from, but I just knew it was there and it wasn't going anywhere.

"SidTheKid. You might've heard me on Money Max's last mixtape," I bragged because it had been my biggest production credit thus far.

"Nah can't say that I've heard that one," he began as he dropped his hand then fingered the hair on his chin, "but I do know good music when I hear it and what I heard the other night was a vibe. You're talented."

At that point I probably should've thanked him or just said anything other than the nothing I was giving, but it took a little longer to find the words after realizing this wasn't his first time over and the last time had been at night.

"Thanks. Alright y'all have a good night," I said quickly because I was trying to get away from them before Daren picked up on the irrational animosity I was feeling towards *her date*.

"Hold up. I've got some really good news for you first. Zeke's cousin Dre wants to meet you. He told him all about you and he let him hear that new beat you sent me last week."

"And?" I asked because by the look of his shea butter wearing ass it didn't look like he had connections to anything but a hotep convention.

"Uh hello. We're only talking about the biggest rapper in the world right now possibly wanting to work with you," she said before lightly pushing my chest to jolt some excitement out of me.

"Wait your cousin is *Dre* Dre? Dre from Canada?" I asked trying not to sound too impressed all of a sudden even though I was.

"Yeah that's my blood and he's in the studio working on new music. I already passed him what I got from D, but he wants you to stop by and introduce yourself," he said before handing me a card with a number and address scribbled on it.

I was speechless again for a second, but I made sure to force out a more genuine sounding thank you this time because I really did mean it.

"Did you need something else?" Daren asked when my feet still hadn't begun walking me over to my own door.

That's when I reminded her that we were supposed to be

doing laundry soon while purposely disregarding the date I had literally begged for all month. Lil' mama would just have to wait though because this situation with Daren was now priority like the mail I had just finished delivering.

"Oh shoot. It is Wednesday, huh? Well me and Zeke were just about to go see a movie," she said as she looked from me to him like she was trying to determine which appointment to keep. I could see her leaning towards him so I decided to take myself out of the running for her time.

"It's cool. I didn't really have much to wash anyway so gone and enjoy yourself," I told her before finally leaving them be.

"Ay what's up with your guard dog?" I heard Zeke ask her through the thin walls after both of our doors were closed.

"He's harmless. Just a good neighbor that looks out for me sometimes."

"That's cool and all, but tell him I got that covered from now on," he said cockily and I swear if it wasn't for the card in my hand that felt like a winning lottery ticket, then I would've came through the wall like Candyman to fuck him up.

And it turned out that I had made the right decision too

because the connect had actually panned out and I got my beats directly into Dre's hands. I was a little overzealous and brought everything I had ever mixed with me, even the old Fisher-Price sounding tracks just in case he found a diamond in the rough that we could use.

He predictably went with a few of my more recent beats, but the fact that even one eventually made his album and became a single was enough to make all that I had sacrificed over the last few years, including living in this dump, worth it.

And of course the next time I saw Daren I tried to play it cool, but I eventually got in her business and questioned her about how long she had been seeing Zeke. The only information she was willing to come off of was that he was a bartender at a club she went to with her friends and that they had just hit it off one night. I couldn't picture it though. I mean I didn't know what her type was, but I couldn't imagine it for real being a nigga like him so I figured he wouldn't be around too long.

I was wrong though because it had been a little over six months now and it didn't look like that nigga was going anywhere. And as much as I hated the idea of her being with him, I couldn't pretend like Zeke wasn't a decent dude from what I did see of him. That extra effort just wasn't there with Daren though and he didn't treat her like he was lucky to have her.

I knew he had a little bread from linking people to his cousin so he definitely should've been taking better care of her especially at this point in the relationship because she loved doing freebies for those reality TV broads and that left her broker than she had to be.

Basically she just deserved more than what he was offering and it fucked me up when I finally realized that I only felt that way because I wanted to be the one to give it to her. Yeah as cliché as it was it took somebody else noticing my friend for me to finally admit that I liked her too, but by that time it was too late for me. She was already in too deep and she really loved that nigga. Without even realizing it I had fumbled my only shot.

It even got to the point that I only really saw her on Wednesdays again just like in the beginning, but I couldn't complain too much because I was always busy too. Working with Dre had led to working with a lot of other artists too, none as big as him yet, but the money was rolling in just the same. My production tag was currently the intro to six songs on the radio and it could be heard at any given time anywhere in the world.

Obviously I was still just getting started but for all intents and purposes a nigga had made it and seemingly came up overnight. I should have been somewhere sitting on top of the world like Mase, but all I could think about was how I was still missing the cherry on top.

Daren was the cherry by the way and besides my mama she was probably my biggest fan. No matter how trash my old beats were she would bob her head and make screwfaces like it was the illest shit she had ever heard. And it made me feel worthy and warm inside knowing that she believed in me.

Yeah she had believed in me enough to talk about me with every person she met out here even her man and that was the biggest reason why I was being blessed with one opportunity after the next. And maybe not being able to enjoy it with her was why I had been unfazed by everything so far.

Our laundry days weren't even really the same after she got with him either though. I didn't necessarily think it was on purpose, but we just kinda did the surface level thing from that point on which I didn't really care for. And then she started joking about me getting ready to drop her soon for my new "Hollywood" friends, but I always told her I wasn't leaving just yet even though I couldn't pretend like the thought hadn't crossed my mind. I was a natural saver anyway so I definitely had more than enough to move to a better spot, but every time I got started on the process I ended up putting it off because I was still waiting around just hoping that Daren would somehow notice that I was in love with her.

And yeah I knew that telling her was the obvious thing to do here, but nah. I wasn't about to put myself out there to be rejected or even worse if she didn't reject me because she maybe wanted to chase the bag that I had finally secured. I knew the old Daren wasn't like that, but the new Daren had been straddling that line because of her new friends and that wasn't how I wanted her. I wanted her to want me the same way that I wanted her. No real rhyme or reason. Just because.

But moving became more than just a far off thought again

when I noticed her doing an extra load of laundry a few weeks ago. At first I didn't think too much of it until I saw her pretreating a stain on a man's shirt. That's when I realized it wasn't her stuff at all. It was Zeke's. And that's also when I told myself that it was officially time to go. It was stupid and probably wouldn't make sense to anybody else, but knowing that he would have that scent on him, the scent that I had never smelled on anybody but me or her, completely ruined it for me.

I liked to think of myself as a patient man, but waiting until the time was right had already taken a toll on me and I couldn't do that shit anymore. I couldn't listen to her laughing in the hallway before they went inside anymore. And I was running out of favorite songs now because I instantly hated whatever music he played to drown out her moans. I had to go.

Ironically I had been seeing more of her again since I told her I'd found a new apartment, but it didn't really mean anything because Zeke was still coming by to knock her headboard into my wall a couple times a week. I took pride in the fact that my headboard always hit it faster and harder than hers did, but it still didn't make up for the fact that I would have given anything to trade places with him.

And it bothered me even more than usual too because I had honestly been too busy and too tired lately to even return the favor which had never happened to me in my life because I always found time to fuck. But between still holding onto my nine to five for health insurance and spending my nights in studios, every free minute I had went to sleeping.

Wednesdays at seven were always the exception daze though but last week had been our last official laundry day together.

There was nothing particularly special about it, but we did say our goodbyes then because the following week would be Valentine's Day and she would be spending it with Zeke. But that was none of my concern anymore since a few days after V day I would be moving out and on to whatever the world had in store for me. Maybe I would even be lucky enough to locate my lost desire for golddiggers again because I hadn't been able to find it since I'd admitted my feelings to myself.

And almost every time I thought about her lately I was reminded of that old song by

Musiq Soulchild, only if *I* would've known the girl next door would've been Daren I swear I would've been more than just nice to her. I would've made her mine too.

For Valentine's Day I had sent my mama one of those big ass Edible Arrangements and a thoughtful card, but she also got a real good laugh at my expense when I finally decided to tell her why I was really moving out this coming weekend. Lorraine Foster was almost thirty years my senior, but she still acted like a teenager when she felt like it and apparently finally admitting that I loved my neighbor who I met up with for laundry once a week brought out her inner kid today.

She knew better than anybody how inconsistent I could be with women so from the beginning she had been accusing me of liking Daren just from the fact that I willingly allowed her in my life week after week. And taking the denial route for the past year and a half had only made my OG more suspicious so I let her have a few minutes to gloat about being right all along.

After that though she reminded me of how scared I had been to ride a bike without training wheels for the first time and every other first in my life that terrified me. I didn't think the bike thing was a good example since I had broken my arm then, but the takeaway was that I had done it. I was scared to fall and I did, but I hadn't let it stop me forever. Shit eventually I got so confident that I was popping wheelies and almost giving her a heart attack every time I got on the thing.

I guess I was supposed to be drawing some kind of parallel to my feelings for Daren, but I didn't think it was the same at all. I could go out right now and break every bone in my body then heal up as good as new, but I had been ducking and dodging another heartbreak because the one caused by my pops abandoning both me and my mama was still raw all these years later.

But all of that was in the past and I was only trying to plan for the future now. I had never been real big on New Year's resolutions outside of still just trying to make it, but after all of the ups and downs from the previous year I told myself that I was coming harder this year because I wanted to be a new man. Cutting through the bullshit though the only thing on the agenda so far was to finally move on from crushing on Daren.

But still for the last month and a half I hadn't done shit and it was the same old-same old and it was about to get worse because today was her first Valentine's Day with him. And I knew that some women loved this day more than their own birthday, but Daren took hers to another level and even left her Christmas tree up just so she could adorn it with red and pink lights and black cherubs. Like clockwork a heart shaped wreath went up on her door the first of February and I heard nothing but love songs coming through the walls.

No doubt she would be doing something special tonight so after work I planned on going out to take my mind off of her being with Zeke next door. But unfortunately for me all of my lil slides were either boo'd up for the holiday or mad that I hadn't returned their calls and texts in a while so it was looking like I would be in the house after all. I wasn't too disappointed though because even with as long as it had been for me, I wasn't necessarily looking to fuck. I just missed having somebody on the other side of my bed while pretending that it was the woman on the other side of the wall who had my heart.

And speaking of her oblivious ass, as soon as I made it upstairs and put my key in the lock I heard her door creaking open. It was more than likely because I had just tossed a package with her name on it in front of it, but I hadn't knocked since I didn't feel like being bothered.

"Don't do it, Daren. Not today," I said pointlessly because she still broke out into song whenever I brought up her stuff.

"Oh yes, wait a minute, Mr. Postman. Wait-hey-hey-hey, Mr. Postman."

"Bruh I'm begging you to stop."

"Please, Mr. Postman, look and see. Is there a letter in your bag for me?"

"Why do you even know this old ass song?"

"'Cause it's been a mighty long time. Since I heard from this boyfriend of mine."

"Now you know that nigga Zeke can barely read let alone write you a letter," I said callously knowing that saying it would stop the singing, but I didn't expect the deep frown that it brought too so I apologized before she followed me inside my apartment.

Whenever I was around her I made sure never to bring him up because I didn't want him to become a part of our conversation so I just pretended like he didn't exist. But lately she had developed a habit of telling me personal things about him like how he preferred talking on the phone because texting could get difficult for him. Yeah it was a low blow and I didn't even really mean it, but I was just upset that the weekend was taking so long to get here because I couldn't wait to get gone for good.

"Why are you acting so grouchy, Sid? It's literally love day and look I got you something," she beamed before revealing a pink and red card from the pocket of her long fluffy robe.

I tried to be cool and take my time putting down my stuff in the living room, but I must've been feeling just as childish as my mama did today because getting a valentine from my valentine had instantly brightened my day.

"Sidney Foster, even though you're leaving soon, you'll always be my favorite neighbor and mailman," she read aloud as I smiled down at the custom card with my full name on it.

"Thanks, but I don't know if I believe you after seeing how excited you get when the Amazon Prime guy gets here."

"No. That's just my little package plaything, but you're a federal employee so we're *super* official and bound by the constitution," she joked awkwardly, but we both looked at each other as the last words left her lips.

"Not anymore. Remember today was my last day." I sat the card down in a safe place then began taking off the layers above my undershirt. "What are you still doing home? I thought you had big Valentine's Day plans?" I asked through a big yawn before she sighed.

"They're plans alright, but they're not exactly big anymore. Zeke's just coming over later after work so we can actually still do laundry at seven if you're not too tired," she said neutrally enough for me to be concerned. I mean this was Daren after all and as far as I knew being lowkey today wasn't her thing even when she was single.

"Alright just let me get a shower and a quick nap in. My dogs are barking," I told her as I slowly slid my feet out of my work shoes. I couldn't even pretend like I would miss my route anymore either because it had been especially rough on me these last few months.

"Hey remind me to give you the number to my new massage place before you go. They hooked me up earlier and I get a bigger discount if I refer friends," she told me casually but being reminded that I was just her friend today of all days stung more than usual.

"Alright. Gone 'head and get back to whatever you were doing. I'll see you in a little while."

"Hey are you okay? You're acting like the Grinch of Valentine's Day," she teased me trying to get me to smile again, but I just let out another yawn.

"Nope. Just tired," I said before heading over to the bathroom and telling her to lock the door on her way out.

I almost felt bad about literally and figuratively shutting her out, but I couldn't exactly come out and say what was bothering me today without messing up her day too. And since I didn't like to focus on shit I couldn't change instead I focused on washing off the day and getting myself fed before falling asleep on the couch.

It was after nine when I got up and saw a missed call from

Daren about an hour before, but she must not have really felt like going after all because usually she would've knocked or even let herself in with my spare key.

I'd had a quick sandwich before taking a nap, but my stomach still did backflips at the scent of whatever she was cooking next door. She usually made enough for me if she knew I was home, but considering it was Valentine's Day I wasn't counting on that since it was supposed to just be a meal for two.

I picked up the phone to see if it was too late to get a pizza delivered, but her familiar double knock made me end the call right as she was letting herself in.

I was hoping that she had brought me a plate after all then laughed to myself about getting excited about the scraps of her food just like I did the scraps of her. But as much as I loved cleaning one of her plates, I wasn't disappointed to look up and see her empty handed. She was literally filling out a pink dress so good that I couldn't do shit but sit up to make sure I wasn't imagining things. I was instantly jealous because it was hugging her body the way I always wanted to.

"Oh good you're up. I know it's getting late, but you still up for laundry?" I could tell that she'd had at least one edible for her anxiety because her eyelids looked heavier than normal, but I didn't mention it.

"Uh…yeah." I stretched then rubbed my eyes one at a time so the other could remain on her before asking the obvious. "What happened to date night?"

"He picked up somebody else's shift or something so he's not coming," she said like she was trying to convince me and herself.

"Then why are you still wearing that?" I asked making

sure not to say anything about his phony alibi.

"Because I had to lose ten pounds just to fit into it. I'm sleeping in this thing and letting you cut me out of it in the morning if I don't pop out first," she said with a forced laugh to cover up the unnecessary mean comment about her size.

"I thought I told you to stop that shit. You look good."

"Thanks. Now come get my bags and I'll make you a big plate when we're done."

"But I'm hungry now."

"No because you'll get too full and go back to sleep just like you did last Fourth of July."

"Well I was drunk because it was my birthday too. Who does laundry on a day off and their birthday?"

"Well it was a Wednesday so we did. You know I'm a creature of habit and I can't function without sticking to my schedule."

"I know, but can I just get a couple bites first? Please Daren," I dragged out her name and whined until she gave in.

"Okay, but you might want to put something on top of those or stop drying your underwear because they aren't doing a good job keeping little Sidney covered." She smirked then let her eyes fall below my waist.

Fresh from waking up, I hadn't even realized that I was only wearing my boxers until she said something, but since I had her attention I slowly adjusted myself because even on soft there was nothing little about Lil Sid.

"Stop letting yourself in then and you won't have to see me like this."

"No. That's the main reason I wanted your spare key in the first place," she said in an uncharacteristically flirtatious way which made me want to match her energy after I grabbed some jeans and a t-shirt.

"Same. But you're always wearing those big ass robes so I never get to see anything."

"Well everybody can't look perfect naked, Sid. And too bad you're leaving because you're going to miss me streaking through the halls after I get my lift for these sad things," she said before cupping her heavy breasts. "And nobody will be able to tell me anything once I save up enough to suck this fat from my waist and put it in my butt."

"Now you know you don't need nothing else back there. You're already sitting on a goldmine," I said candidly because what she was already holding was perfect for her small but chunky frame. She just lived on Instagram and wouldn't stop comparing herself to those girls who were taller and slimmer models.

"You really think so?" she asked as she looked back at it over her shoulder in my mirror.

"Yeah I don't think you need any of that. You're fine just the way you are, Daren." I had put on my jeans, but I stalled pulling the shirt over my head so that I could see her reaction to my compliment which I knew she wouldn't just accept at face value.

"C'mon. Even Zeke told me another twenty pounds would do me some good."

"And another inch to his hairline would do his big ass forehead some good," I cracked on his locs that were starting to thin out.

Yeah see that was yet another reason why that nigga had to go. Because I would never tell her to change anything and I would be damned if I never got to experience the natural body that had my dick standing at attention since she'd started wearing clothes her size. She had always been cute, but it wasn't until then that I could make out the shape that she had hidden from me and the rest of the world. I wanted to kick myself for being around her so much and never taking the time to really look at all she came with.

"You better leave my baby alone," she said as she led the way back over to her spot, but I had one last thing to say.

"Forget about him. I don't want you listening to that noise. Listen to me. There's somebody for you that'll accept you for exactly who you are. No nips or tucks. Just you."

"That's sweet to say, but you don't have to lie just because we're friends."

I sighed at her using the F word again and because even though my nap had given me an energy boost, I still didn't have enough to try to convince her to think otherwise so I just let it go then took a seat while she made me a small plate. I made small talk by asking about her mama.

"She's alright. She's been telling everybody how good therapy is working out for me, but little does she know it's really just you and these drugs," she said before pointing to the container that I'd refilled the other day on her countertop.

"You're saying that like we're Bobby and Whitney or

something. It's just a little ass legal gummy to relax."

"Well tell that to the woman who thinks Nyquil is over the counter heroin," she said making me smile at how funny her folks could be.

I had always noticed that the layout to our apartments were mirror images of each other, but hers looked neater and more feminine with the neutral and pastel colored décor. I had just plopped a big ass TV, a couch, and my home studio equipment in mine so it didn't exactly look like home sweet home. I planned on changing that with the new place though, but I didn't know where to start.

I thought about asking for her help before I remembered that I was supposed to be leaving her and all that came with her right here with Zeke. Only that was easier said than done especially since there was a different vibe to her tonight. And granted she had long stopped being as shy as she was with me when we met, I couldn't put my finger on this new feeling. Or rather I could, but I just knew I had to be losing it because there was no way that Daren was trying me like that.

I mean I had kinda figured she had a small thing for me in the beginning, but she was long over that and now it seemed like she only looked at me a certain way. She had seen me with other women and even without a shape up so she was too comfortable now. But I knew it was a done deal when she started trying to hook me up with her old friend who had moved here from Vermont. I had met her a couple times and she was cool, but she wasn't Daren.

I knew I wasn't too off base with my hunch though when instead of handing me the plate she decided to cut off a bite of steak and potatoes then put it up to my lips. I accepted it and her direct eye contact as I chewed then swallowed the best thing I had eaten all year so far. And the fact that it had been meant for Zeke made it taste even better.

"Good?"

"Always is," I told her before asking for one more perfect bite just like that one. She indulged me with a smile then wrapped the rest up for later. And from the way that she slowly wiped my mouth with the pad of her thumb I knew that this laundry date was about to be a little different from all the others.

I carried everything down with a smile of my own because on the advice of my mama I was about to finally go for it, rejection be damned. Zeke not coming had given us another shot at what I hoped wouldn't be goodbye anymore. And no matter what happened I would be cool because I would never have to wonder what if.

Usually when we came to the laundry room, we would immediately bust out a deck of cards because I brought out her competitive side since I beat her most of the time. Sometimes we would even stay past the time it took the clothes to dry because she would refuse to leave until she beat me at least once. It was funny because even though I had taught her all of my tricks, she just didn't have Spades instincts and I blamed that on her family being from white ass New England.

"I'm glad we got to do this final rematch because it's crazy how much you were cheating me last week," she accused me after we had both loaded our machines.

It was always my job to bring the cards so I pretended to look when she asked for them, but I had purposely left them upstairs because once and for all I wanted to get some answers out of her. I wanted to see if maybe she was starting to look at me again how I had been looking at her.

"You want me to go get them?" she offered after I looked around another minute.

"Nope. I guess we don't need them."

I took a seat up on the countertop, but she chose to stand and lean next to me. That's when I noticed that she had traded in her heels for a comfortable pair of pink furry slides, but she was still wearing the fuck out of that dress.

"What are we gonna do then?"

"Talk. And I mean I don't want to get all in your business like that, but you're not really buying Zeke's working late excuse are you?" I asked getting straight to the point since we were on borrowed time now. I knew I had her undivided attention for the next hour and change and I planned on using it wisely.

"It's not an excuse. I heard his coworkers in the background so I know he's not with somebody else if that's what you're thinking," she said sounding defensive.

"Even still. He knows how much today means to you so he should've been here. If you were my girl you definitely wouldn't be alone on a special night like this," I said then tried to rein it in because I was going too hard too soon.

"But I thought you said if the mail is still delivered then it's not even a real holiday," she reminded me about how cynical I usually was because the only Cupid I acknowledged was the Cupid Shuffle.

"Well yeah Valentine's day is a made up holiday and it doesn't have meaning for *me*, but women love it and if a man loves a woman then--"

"Then he should love it too, right?"

"That's not what I was about to say at all. He should just make an effort to make sure she enjoys her meaningless day because it's not hurting anything to make her feel appreciated. We get away with being bums all year round so if a man can't get his act together for this one day then maybe there's a bigger problem there."

"It's nothing like that. Zeke cares about me. He's just grinding really hard right now and saving just like we are. And I don't expect him to go all out wasting money on flowers, cards, and candy just because I'm a hopeless romantic. That's not real life."

"Yeah it is. I was broker than broke in high school and I still managed to shake shit up with a twenty for my girl back then, but you know him better than me so you're probably right," I told her after checking the time on my phone. Thankfully it was moving slowly so far.

I almost felt bad for planting seeds of doubt in her relationship, but it wasn't like I was saying something that wasn't true. Zeke had majorly dropped the ball by not showing up so I was about to pick that shit up and not stop running until I reached the end zone.

"So what do you think this bigger problem is if it's not money?" she asked right on cue because I knew she valued my opinion since I always gave it to her straight.

"You know what? Nevermind. It's not really my place."

"No tell me. I don't want to be walking around looking stupid if you can see something that I can't," she prodded before I sighed hard like it pained me to say it.

"He doesn't really want you like that, Daren. And that doesn't mean you're not a catch. It just means you gotta get caught by somebody who actually wants to catch you, a good dude," I told her genuinely as I looked down at the fret that she couldn't hide even in her deep brown eyes.

"I already have one."

"Well somebody needs to tell that to the sad look in your eyes then because they ain't get the memo yet."

"There is no sad look in my eyes. I've just been up since six this morning getting ready for tonight," she said before complaining about how long it took to do her hair and how that made her late for her massage, nail and wax appointments.

"Yeah all of that to get ready for him, but you expect me to believe that you don't think you're worth a real date let alone flowers, cards, and candy?" That shut her up for a hot second but not for good.

"It's not about my worth. You don't get it Sid because you're used to walking away from situations the first time they don't make you happy." I knew what she was doing, trying to shift the focus on my lack of meaningful relationships, but I was already two steps ahead of her.

"So then you are admitting that you're not happy with him?"

"That's not what I said."

"But it's what you meant, right? And why stay if you're not happy?"

"Because I just…Whatever. I'm not in the mood to be by myself right now," she said dropping all pretenses and I could see the sense of relief fall over her.

"But you're not by yourself. You got me, every Wednesday and more if you need."

"Not anymore remember?" she pointed out about my upcoming move and for the first time I felt bad about it. "Besides I'm not trying to be a burden on anybody."

"C'mon Daren. You're way too cute to be a burden." It was a quick slip of the tongue, but I didn't take it back because I'd meant it.

"What are you doing?" she asked curiously with a slightly tilted head.

"What?"

"You're acting different tonight."

"Me? I feel like you're the one who's being different."

"Different like how?"

"Since when do you feed me and look me in my eyes and shit?"

"I let you taste food when I'm cooking all the time, Sid."

"Yeah but tonight was weird because you were being flirty too, like you were thinking about putting something else in my mouth," I accused her straightforwardly with a lick of my lips as I allowed myself to look at her breasts.

The strapless bra she had on was working overtime to give her ample cleavage, but I wanted nothing more than to relieve it of its duties with my hands. "Am I right?"

"Hold up." She picked up my chin. "It's way too early for April Fools' Day and trust me. These are not the kind of packages that you're used to handling, Mr. Postman."

"I don't care. I like how they're wrapped," I teased her as I played with the strap on her dress.

"Well according to you I'm sad so you wouldn't dare take advantage of me in my vulnerable state, would you?"

"Don't give me so much credit. And I'm feeling a little vulnerable today too. That's why I've been trying to get your *shy when it's convenient* ass to make the first move," I told her forwardly then watched closely to see how she would respond, but

she just looked down at her feet
and spoke softly.

"I thought I already did," she
said so low that I had to asked her
to repeat herself. "Sid, Zeke didn't
cancel our date tonight. I told him
not to come over because when I
got up this morning, I realized
that I would rather spend one last
night with you instead."

"So you're missing out on
Valentine's Day with your man
because you wanted to do laundry
with me one last time…or
something else?" I asked strictly
for clarification purposes because
I wasn't going to do anything
until she gave me the green light.

"More than laundry…if you want to," she said while keeping her eyes focused on the floor. I could tell that the conversation taking an X-rated turn had her retreating back into her shell, but before she could get all the way inside I reached out and pulled her over so that she could stand between my legs.

The second I put my hands on her bare shoulders I felt her trembling from my touch so I didn't go any lower. I knew she wasn't the type to step out on her relationship so I decided to give her a chance to back out before we went too far.

"You sure this is what you want?" She nodded before I could finish asking.

"I don't think I've ever wanted anything more than this." She stood on the balls of her feet to reach my lips, but it still wasn't enough. And before I could even attempt to meet her halfway, she had grabbed hold of my neck and brought me down to her.

I had dreamed about something like this happening for months on end, but the fact that it was now a reality was almost scary because I'd thought that my imagination was as good as it got only I had underestimated her.

The long buildup of waiting for our first kiss had the neurons in my brain firing off in a way that I'd never felt before. My instincts wanted me to rush it, but looking in her eyes had me slowing down my pace and trying to savor the moment. Savor feeling her full lips sensually wrestling with mine and feeling nothing between us but our clothes which I decided had to go after a little while. She grinned through our kiss as I went to slide down her bra.

"Wait. We have two empty apartments right upstairs. I think we can wait until the clothes dry before we start opening packages."

"Why should we wait? It's not like anybody can hear us down here."

"Because. Somebody might come in."

"But nobody ever comes in," I exaggerated since it did happen every now and then, but they didn't usually stay once they saw us playing cards and listening to music.

"You came down here wearing this because you wanted me to notice you, Daren. So I'm doing it. I'm noticing everything and now I want it right here in our spot," I told her as I went in for another kiss. "You really never thought about what it would be like in here?"

"I did last week. Like in a *this would be the cheesiest porno ever* kind of way."

"Oh that's how you thought about it?"

"Well how did you think about it?"

Instead of answering I made her back up some so that I could get off the counter to show her, but she went backwards until her butt bumped the still spinning washing machine. She had gotten better at faking confidence since we met, but I guess it was harder to do with a hard dick staring her down and threatening to impale her.

I honestly didn't care where the hell we did it. I just wanted to be able to put my mouth on her body as soon as possible to try to make up for lost time. But I could tell that even though she was worried about being caught at the same time she was turned on by the thought of it too.

Without asking I put my hand on top of her heart and just like I expected it was racing. Mine sounded like a percussion instrument in my chest, but I took in a big gulp of air as I undid the tie on the back of her dress.

The straps fell forward and a light tug on her bra freed her breasts for me. I barely allowed them to fall from the constraints of the cups before I had one in my hand and the other between my lips.

"Ow. Not so hard."

"My bad." I released her tender nipple then drew in the other one, but I controlled my appetence this time because I was already enjoying learning her body.

I had been studying it for so long that I knew I could probably ace the test on the first try, but a little extra credit never hurt either.

I went to take off her panties and maybe hold onto them for a keepsake but found that there was nothing for me to remove because she wasn't wearing any. Nothing but soft, bare skin greeted my fingers underneath her dress and then it quickly parted for me to meet her clit.

"Ohhh," she whimpered out as I ran the tips back and forth along her slick slit then teased the sensitive bud with her wetness.

I still couldn't wrap my mind around the fact that my fingers were actually pushing inside of her and the hot, wet suction of her walls drew me in deeper with every swipe of her clit.

"Mm. You gonna do it like that on my dick too?" I asked but got nothing but incoherent words and expletives from her. She barely ever cursed, but the closer she got to coming the more she sounded like a sailor.

"Fuck. Oh my god. Sidney. I think I'm...I'm..."

"Let it out. Tell me how good it feels," I encouraged her while continuing to rub her in a circular motion. Her hips bucked back against me, eager to get the next strokes until electricity shot through her body and she gushed into my palm.

"Siiid. What are you doing to me?" she whined as I finally

slowed down because I wanted my face to get in on this too.

"Nothing yet," I promised then grabbed her by the waist and bent at the knees.

"What are you doing?" she asked worried as I tried to pick her up, but she kept herself grounded.

"What does it look like? I'm putting you up here so I can eat it."

"But you can't just go picking up a woman like me out of the blue. I need a warning," she joked still holding onto her fast beating heart.

"Man if you don't get your big fine ass up here and let me

fucking taste you already," I told her before lifting her then plopping her back down.

Her legs naturally spread allowing me a sneak peek at the tsunami I had created before I quickly dropped to my knees then lifted the dress above her hips.

A few feet away her phone vibrated over on the counter, but I ignored it then draped her big soft legs over my shoulders.

"Sid. Wait let me--" her sentence was cut short when my tongue tapped her clit.

"Daren, if you're not telling me to go faster or slower then I don't want to hear it right now, alright?"

"But--"

"But nothing. I know you can't help it sometimes, but for once I just need you to not overthink a situation. Just enjoy this shit because we've both been wanting it to happen for way too long," I said with authority as I kissed the inside of her thighs.

"Okay. You're right." She opened up more for me then encouraged me to continue by rubbing the back of my head.

And even though my bare knees were scraping the concrete floor through my ripped jeans, her warm brown thighs wrapped around my head made me feel at home so I got as comfortable as possible since I planned on being down there for a while.

I sucked and licked her clit with the intensity that I wanted to use on her sensitive nipples and got no complaints this time. But it might've also had something to do with her turning into jelly as my fingers went deeper than the Pacific at the same time since I was trying to make up for all of the Wednesdays that I could've been doing this instead of playing cards.

"Damn. How could you keep this away from me all this time?" I asked after stopping for a second to admire her sweet essence, but I got no answer from her. I did, however, hear loud footsteps coming down the stairs to the basement like they were headed our way.

I gave her pussy one last slurp before standing to my feet then quickly tried to fix her dress that was halfway hanging off of her. She had been close to coming again though so her only concern was why I had stopped until she heard the door to the laundry room opening.

"Sid! I told you," she whispered worriedly as whoever it was came in sounding like they were dragging a heavy hamper behind them.

"Don't worry. I got you." I tied the straps of her dress as best as I could, but I kept her legs open enough for me to get my fingers back in when I realized that our guest couldn't see us because they were using the machines on the other side.

"You need to tell your son to keep up with his clothes," a man's voice said to somebody on the phone and I recognized it as the dude who lived underneath me in 4B. "Nah he's only my son when he's behaving."

I guess the plan was to stay quiet until he was gone, but our washer had other plans as it finally stopped with a loud ding which startled both me and Daren.

"Ay who's over there? Bae let me call you back," he said like he was getting ready to square up.

"It's Sid. What's up Matt?" I asked as casually as possible because my fingers were still slowly fucking Daren and my hand over her mouth could only do so much.

"Nothing. Sleepier than a motherfucker and my kid waited until after his mama left for work to tell me he's out of clean shirts for school."

"Bet his lil bad ass did that on purpose," I joked because every time I ran across them in the building I was thankful that I lived above them and not the other way around.

"Man hell yeah. Ay Sid you got any shorties?" he asked curiously out of the blue.

"None that I know of." I focused back on Daren then saw her cut her eyes at me before they almost rolled in the back of her head at the pressure I started applying to her clit.

"That's what's up. I know you about to be taking down every bad singing bitch in LA now that you got your deal," he said sounding like he wished he could trade places with me.

"Nah. It's not even like that."

"Word, you too good for the hoes now?" I almost laughed at how he asked but kept a straight face for Daren.

"Yeah my taste is changing." She raised an eyebrow, but I just bent down and kissed the spot between her eyes.

"Is it niggas now? Because I know the music industry works fast but not that fast," he asked seriously and I had to laugh at that before telling him that he had me fucked up.

I slipped up and dropped my hand from her mouth for a second before a small moan escaped her trembling lips.

"Mm hey Matt," she said

recovering quickly then thinking on her feet.

"Oh whaddup Daren," he said coming over to speak to her.

I felt her tense up at his presence, but luckily my back was to him and he couldn't see where my hand was. She was doing a bad job of pretending like she was on my phone especially since the screen wasn't even turned on, but it wasn't even necessary. I would've laughed if I wasn't so turned on thinking about how much wetter she felt each time I stroked her.

"I should've known your ass was in here with him. Ay Blood, you need to quit playing and jump on that. That's a good woman right there," he said like he hadn't just been encouraging me to fuck off with other women.

"I'm trying, but she's already got a man," I told him honestly and felt her pussy thump around my fingers at the mention of Zeke.

I couldn't tell if I was doing that good of a job or if the excitement from having an unknowing bystander witnessing her pussy being played with was the culprit, but either way she was loving it.

"Ay y'all gon be down here a while?" Matt asked pulling out his phone to set an alarm for the washer. Everybody in the building knew that you had to stay close by or else your shit was liable to get stolen.

"Yeah these machines keep fucking up and I think I'll need a second dry. What about you, Daren? Is your stuff still wet too?" I asked impishly while turning back to see her teeth cruelly biting down on her bottom lip so I could only get a nod out of her.

Matt was so into his phone that he was still oblivious to what was happening right in front of his eyes, but we still enjoyed the audience regardless.

"Alright bet. Watch my shit. I'll be back to put it in the dryer," he said before suddenly hurrying out because of whatever he had seen on his phone.

The second he was gone and the door had slammed shut, I had my jeans and boxer briefs at my ankles and I was lining up my head to enter her. She was already on the verge of coming again so I worked quickly before I fucked up her orgasm.

Just like me she really must've decided to do this on a whim because neither of us had come prepared with protection. And yeah I could've gone up to get one, but I wasn't doing it if she didn't make me because I wanted to feel her and nothing but her wrapped around me.

"You still make him wrap it up?" I asked as if her answer would make a difference. It was irresponsible as fuck but before she could even finish nodding I had dove in, thick head first.

Instantly I regretted being so ambitious in my fantasies because pussy like this wasn't nothing to play with. She may not have known how to play Spades, but apparently Vermont pussy hit different than the west coast and Midwest that I'd had so far.

I had given her too much to start with so she inched backwards towards the wall, but I slowly pulled her back down on most of it because I was already addicted to that feeling.

"Ay Daren, the dick you want is down here so why are you all the way up there?"

The sound of my voice in her ear must've pushed her over the edge because she held onto the sides of the machine tightly as she threw her head back and gushed on my dick. Damn I wasn't gonna make it.

"Fuck. Look at how you're dripping down my legs and shit already. Who told you it was okay to drip down my legs like this?" I asked rhetorically glover the loud wet clapping sounds we were now making.

"I'm...sorry," she struggled to get out, still trying to keep it together, but it was pointless. After all of the foreplay and the mindfuck of almost being caught, she was officially spent so there was nothing left for me to do but fill her up.

"No you're not. You're loving this shit." I couldn't reach her nipples from this position so instead I put my face in the crook of her neck and gently sucked there as I fucked her with all the fire inside of me.

Her hips started to slow wine with me, but I pumped faster to make sure she couldn't keep up and just had to take it. She could have it however she wanted when she got on top, but this was still my turn and all I wanted was her sitting there satisfied full of my dick.

I tried to drag it out as long as I could, but her clinging to me and her head on my shoulder and biting my arm to keep her groans contained made the heat in my balls churn.

When it got to the point that I was about to come, we were in dangerous territory because I didn't care who the fuck came in now. The pope could've walked in here and I wasn't stopping until I felt those familiar waves washing over me.

"Fuck Daren. You feel so…" My moan got caught in my throat like a hiccup as my body experienced some shit that felt so good it had to be illegal somewhere.

We had barely finished and I felt like I was already strung out on her because I didn't want to leave her body yet. I struggled between trying to catch my breath and kiss her deeply before I just said fuck it and breathed hard with my lips still touching hers.

"Damn you're amazing," I told her when I finally felt like I had enough air in my lungs again.

"You're not so bad yourself."

She placed a sweet kiss on my chin before I slowly helped her down and get steady on her shaky legs.

We had made a big mess up there, but I let her go up first while I cleaned it up then finally threw our clothes in the dryers.

Her door was slightly askew when I got up to our floor so I knew she wanted me to go to her spot. But I wasn't a vampire so I was coming in whether I was invited or not since something that belonged to me now was inside.

I found her in the bathroom on the toilet with her head resting on her fist.

"Damn you look tired. Fuck happened to you?" I asked her before closing the door behind me and she half smiled, but I could sense now that the reality of what we had just done was sinking in she wasn't really in the mood to play.

"So what do we do now Sid?" she asked me as I took a seat on the side of her tub. "You're moving out in two days and I still have a boyfriend."

I felt my brain winding down from the long day and the sensory overload I'd had just a few minutes before. The most obvious answer to her question didn't require much thought though and it was a solution to both of those dilemmas.

"Come with me."

"What?"

"You heard me Daren."

"I did, but you know it's not that simple."

"You love him?" I asked straightforwardly because I was sure I knew the answer. She sighed hard.

"I care about him a lot, Sid," she said which hurt a lot, but I knew I wanted no regrets tonight so I soldiered on.

"You love me?" I asked with less confidence this time because I knew her answer could make or break me.

"If it's not love, then it's something very close to it," she said softly before pulling me and my lips in for the sweetest kiss we'd ever had. We both smelled like drying sweat, but underneath it I could still make out the scent of her detergent and that made me happy.

"You don't know how good it feels to hear you say that."

"I will know if you tell me you feel the same," she said looking at my eyes like she was unsure and I couldn't fight off the smile that took over every inch of my face.

"Feel the same? Daren before you got here I used to do laundry *maybe* twice a month. I haven't had a full load since you moved in, but every Wednesday there I was in that dingy ass basement just to have an excuse to spend time with you," I said with my full chest because it was finally dawning on me just how long I'd had feelings for her and it was long before Zeke came in the picture.

"My feelings for you will always run deeper than you know, but just believe me when I say that I've **been** loving you," I told her honestly, but I still saw some doubt in her eyes which was confirmed by her words.

"But how do I know that this isn't just you liking the idea of stealing me from him?"

"Because you can't steal what was already yours. If you need time then you got it, but just like I was here first I guarantee that I'mma be the last man standing when it comes to you. And now you know everything so all that's left to do is to choose me, Daren," I pleaded with her as I swept away a few stray hairs that had gotten stuck to her damp forehead.

"I really want to Sid, but you're asking a lot of me right now and I just don't know if I can give it all to you so fast."

"You're right. It is a lot. But at the end of the day all I want from you is to see you tomorrow and every tomorrow after that. I don't want to move or be anywhere else if you're not there so just come with me and we'll figure out everything else as we go, alright?" I promised by giving her my pinky and my word because she knew how much it meant to me.

"And if for whatever reason you're thinking about saying no, I just want you to know that our new spot comes with a washer and dryer inside of it so we'll never get caught again unless that's just something you're into now," I said just to make her laugh and my heart nearly took flight when she leaned over to give me another kiss.

"Alright. Geesh Sid. Calm down. I'll come, but we're not getting married," she said sarcastically with a smile and I almost frowned before I remembered that I had said the same thing to her when she was talking too much the day we met.

"We're not getting married *yet*," I told her with emphasis on "yet" to make it clear that I could definitely see us there someday soon.

"But I am going out tomorrow morning to buy you all the flowers, cards, and candy that

I can find because I'm not Zeke and I don't ever want you to think that I don't appreciate you being my valentine."

"Well thank you for that, but right now I'm a little more concerned with how we're gonna get this dress off of me," she said playfully because the material was clinging to her damp skin.

I wasn't worried though because I had a feeling it would be so wet that it would slide right off of her after what I planned on doing for the rest of the night.

FOLLOW ME

Thanks for reading! If you don't want to miss out on any updates about future works of mine then find me on all social media platforms as TanSaidWhat.

Visit www.tanzaniaglover.com

And if the cover art took your breath away as much as it did mine, check out the talented artists at NewLevelsGraphics! Thank you so much for bringing this couple to life!

THANK YOUS

I said that I was done writing dissertations to my family and friends in this section so I'll try to keep this brief especially since my love for them has remained the same since the first time I did this. But I do want to say that I feel like the luckiest person in the world to be able to go on this journey with people who genuinely love and care for me. Because of the immense amount of love and support that I receive from them, I get to do the thing I love most in the world and I'm forever grateful for it.